Sky Pony Press books may be purchased in bulk at special discounts for sales promotion, corporate gifts, fund-raising, or educational purposes. Special editions can also be created to specifications. For details, contact the Special Sales Department, Sky Pony Press, 307 West 36th Street, 11th Floor, New York, NY 10018 or info@skyhorsepublishing.com.

Sky Pony® is a registered trademark of Skyhorse Publishing, Inc.®, a Delaware corporation.

Visit our website at www.skyponypress.com.

10 9 8 7 6 5 4 3 2 1

Manufactured in China, February 2013
This product conforms to CPSIA 2008

Library of Congress Cataloging-in-Publication Data

Dokey, Cameron.
  Zack's story / written by Cameron Dokey ; illustrated by Craig Orback.
      p. cm. -- (Boys camp ; bk. 1)
  Summary: "Zack is finally attending summer camp, a dream he's always had. But he quickly realizes that the wilderness has unexpected twists and turns and he must band together with his friends to stay safe and have fun"-- Provided by publisher.
  ISBN 978-1-62087-528-5 (hardcover : alk. paper) [1. Camps--Fiction. 2. Friendship--Fiction.] I. Orback, Craig, ill. II. Title.
  PZ7.D69743Zac 2013
  [Fic]--dc23
                              2012041023.

ISBN: 978-1-62087-528-5

Book 1
Zack's Story

Written by Cameron Dokey
Illustrated by Craig Orback

**Every boy has
a great story.**

Sky Pony Press
New York

Have fun. Make friends. Be yourself.

Hello, New Camper!

All of us at Camp Wolf Trail are looking forward to welcoming you on July 10. We've got a great summer ahead of us.

Pretty soon you'll be packing your gear for your two weeks here at camp. Since this will be your first summer at Wolf Trail, you're probably excited and curious— and maybe even a little nervous—about what to expect, especially if this is your first time away from home.

Well, first of all, don't worry. Camp is fun. And here at Wolf Trail, we've been sharing the fun with kids like you for more than fifty years. As soon as you arrive, counselors and returning campers will help you settle into your cabin. The cabins are simple, screened-in, wooden structures that are scattered like acorns throughout the woods.

At Camp Wolf Trail, counselors and campers of different ages are assigned to groups called "clusters," and every cluster chooses its own goofy name and its own silly signature move. Together, you and your cluster will take turns doing communal chores, like setting the table or washing the dishes for eighty hungry monkeys (also known as the campers, counselors, and camp staff). You and your cluster will compete against other clusters during our once-a-week camp theme days, including the Oddball Championships. Past themes have been Martian Day, Rock Star Day, Backwards Day, Crazy Cool Racing Day, and Chicken-of-the-Woods Day.

Every day, there are lots of activities to choose from: swimming in clear, cool Evergreen Lake, boating, canoeing, arts and crafts, hiking, sports, and trail blazing. At night, everyone at camp gathers around a fire for songs, stories, jokes, and reflection. And each week, you and your fellow campers and counselors will go off on a wilderness backpacking trek, hiking into the woods with only what you'll need to survive for two nights and three days: water, food, sleeping bags, and flashlights to light the way through the piney forest. You'll hike to breezy overlooks, discover secret, hidden swimming spots, cook over a campfire, sleep out under the stars, and listen to owls hooting in the woods.

You are in for quite an adventure! So, pack your enthusiasm and your sense of humor, along with your socks, and come to Camp Wolf Trail. We are ready for the fun to begin, and we know that you are too. See you soon!

From,
All of us here at Camp Wolf Trail

Packing List

Due to our simple camp lifestyle, and our even-more-rustic wilderness trips, anything you bring may get wet, dirty, lost, or all three combined. So, leave the special stuff at home.

Do bring:
Daily camp supplies
- ☐ Shorts and T-shirts for warm weather
- ☐ Clothes for cooler temperatures (fleece clothing is good for camping because it dries quickly)
- ☐ Socks (wool is good for hiking because it also dries quickly)
- ☐ Hiking shoes or boots for trips, and everyday shoes for camp (be sure to break in new boots or shoes before you get here!)
- ☐ Old sneakers/water shoes for canoeing and creek hikes
- ☐ Swimming gear: suit, sunscreen, towel
- ☐ Sheets, blanket, and pillow for your bunk in camp
- ☐ Bathroom items: towel, toothbrush, toothpaste, shampoo, soap (although we've noticed that some campers' soaps don't get used too often!)

Wilderness trip supplies
- ☐ The basics: a comfortable backpack, lightweight sleeping bag, roll-up camping pad, mess kit (plate, cup, fork, and spoon) water bottle, flashlight with extra batteries, waterproof poncho
- ☐ Optional: camping knife (check it in with your counselor

when you arrive), camping pillow, compass, hat, bandanna

☐ If you wear glasses, bring a cord to hold them safely around your neck, so you don't lose them when boating or rock climbing.

Other optional items

☐ Good books

☐ Portable games such as cards and cribbage, crossword puzzles

☐ Paper, stamps, envelopes, pen, addresses (your parents and friends will want to hear from you!)

☐ Art supplies, journal, nature guides, binoculars, musical instrument (if it's not too fragile), or other hobby supplies

☐ Pocket money (no more than $20, though)

Please **do not bring** any electronics or a cell phone. They don't survive getting wet, dirty, or lost. And besides, who needs them? You'll be hiking in the woods and swimming in the lake most of the time. Who would you text? A squirrel? A fish? Enjoy being free of screens (except the kind that keeps bugs out) for two weeks!

Chapter One

So, Zack Wilson thought, almost laughing at himself, *I've been at Camp Wolf Trail, what? Ten minutes? And already I'm having an adventure.*

Zack looked at the rough map in his hands. He wasn't *lost* in the woods, exactly. He just didn't know where he was.

"I'll swap you this map for your gear," the counselor, Carlos, had said with a grin, right after Zack waved good-bye to his parents as they drove away. "Your mission is to find Birch Cabin, your home while you're here. Have fun on your map challenge. And don't worry: Someone will always be tracking you. Oh, and welcome to Camp Wolf Trail!"

So Zack had set out, striding along the path through the shady woods, taking deep breaths of the pine-scented air, his thumbs hooked through the straps of his backpack, his legs feeling strong and sure. His whole life, he'd dreamed of walking through the woods all on his own like this. And the hike was great, just the way he'd always imagined hiking would be—up until now.

Now, there was trouble dead ahead. The big path split into two smaller trails. But the map showed the path dividing into *three* trails, and it was the trail on the far left—the one that didn't seem to exist in real life—that led to Birch Cabin.

Knowing how to read a map was important. Zack knew that from studying his favorite book in the entire universe, *The Outdoor Adventure Guide*. The *Guide* told almost everything there was to know about the great outdoors: how to build a shelter or start a fire; how to use a compass or navigate by the stars.

Zack could feel the book, hard and flat against his back, inside his backpack.

Zack had read *The Outdoor Adventure Guide* from cover to cover, over and over. He practically had the chapter on map reading memorized. But this was his first experience actually *using* a map to get where he wanted to go.

It was harder than it looked, particularly now that Zack was deep in the woods, and especially when the map didn't match the path. *I guess this is the challenging part of the map challenge,* Zack thought. Zack could feel his hands starting to sweat. He wasn't scared, but he couldn't help thinking he must have gone wrong somewhere. *Stay calm,* he told himself. He knew what the *Guide* said about getting scared:

A little scare isn't always a bad thing. It can help you pay attention. It can keep you on your toes. But it's hard to think straight when you panic. If you get too scared, you can put yourself in danger. So remember: It's okay to just stop walking.

Well, Zack thought. *I can handle the* stop part. *It's which way to* go *that's the problem.*

At least there were no distractions, none of the city sounds that Zack was used to. No horns honking or sirens blaring. No radios turned up too loud. Instead, the wind made a kind of restless sound, moving through the tree branches way up high, and every once in a while a bird called.

Oof! Wham!

Something hit Zack in the back. Hard.

"Aaah!" Zack cried. He spun around to see a kid backing up so fast that Zack was afraid the guy would trip over his own feet and fall over backward.

"Oh, man," the kid said. "I ran smack into you, didn't I? Sorry, sorry. I didn't watch where I was going. I mean, I *did*. But I was trying to look at my compass *and* the map *and* the path at the same time and I . . . "

"It's okay," Zack said, breaking into the tumble of words. The kid talked so fast Zack was almost out of breath just listening. "I'm not hurt. You just surprised me. That's all."

"Really?" the other kid asked. He stopped and stood still. "You're not mad? Not at *all*?"

Zack shrugged. "Nope."

The new kid was as tall and skinny as a telephone pole. He looked like maybe he should be wearing glasses, but he wasn't. In one hand, the kid carried a compass, and in the other hand he had a map just like the one Zack was holding.

"Hey, are you looking for Birch Cabin?" Zack asked.

"Yeah!" the other kid cried. "I'm Jim." He shoved his compass in his pocket and grabbed Zack's hand and shook it hard, pumping Zack's arm up and down. "Some of the other guys might call me Jimmy, but don't pay any attention. That was last year. This year, it's Jim all the way. I'm eleven now."

"Me too. I'm Zack," Zack said. The

handshake was over, but Zack's whole arm tingled. "So, you've been here at camp before, right?"

"Yep," Jim nodded. "We do some super-cool stuff: canoeing, mountain treks and rock climbing, Oddball Championships. You'll have a great time. Once we find the cabin and the rest of the guys, of course. You'll like the guys. They're from all over the place, all over the *globe*, really. Like Erik's from Norway, and—"

"Whoa, whoa, whoa," Zack interrupted. "You said, 'once we find the cabin.' You mean you don't you know where Birch Cabin is?"

Jim shook his head. "No clue. I wasn't in Birch last year. They move us around. Plus, maps and I do *not* get along. I see one, and my brain goes *Ffzzzztt*. I think all maps are made by alien life forms. Which means they don't show life on *this* planet at all. The aliens just want you to think they do, so they can lure you into a trap. Take this map for instance." Jim waved his map in the air. "It shows a place where the path divides, but into *three* branches, not *two*."

"Yeah, I know," said Zack. "My map shows that too."

"Bummer," Jim said. "So, you and I were given the same map. Other guys in Birch Cabin got different maps with easier trails to follow. Ah, well . . ."

Jim stretched his long, lanky self on the ground and propped his head against the trunk of a tree that had fallen so that it was lying sideways, its upended roots uphill and its branches downhill.

Zack had to grin. His new friend seemed to have only two speeds: 100 miles per hour and zero.

"Might as well rest until our tracker comes to help us," Jim said. "Anyway, I think better when I'm lying down, like this tree. Nice of it to fall next to the path, so's I can use it for a pillow. Looks like it just fell yesterday, because . . ."

"Hey!" Zack cut in. "Maybe that's it!

Maybe the tree *just* fell, and it's blocking the third trail, and *that's* why we can't see it."

Jim leapt up, all in one move. "Only one way to find out," he said.

Zack and Jim scrambled over the tree trunk and batted their way through the fallen tree's tangled branches.

"Ta da!" cheered Zack when they were standing free of the branches. He pointed ahead, where a path twisted down to the left. "Look, Jim. It's the third trail. The fallen tree *did* hide it from us. Come on! Let's go!"

"Hang on!" said Jim. "How do you know this is the path we should take?"

"Check it out," said Zack. He showed Jim his map. "Trust the map. See? That trail to the right looked pretty good in person, but on the map . . ."

He traced his finger along the path to the right. "It dead-ends before you go very far. And if we followed the center path . . ."

Now Zack ran his finger along the path

that ran straight up the middle. "We'd end up in something called the Marsh."

"So that means . . ." Jim breathed.

"Yep," Zack nodded. He traced the left path with his finger. It zigzagged through the trees for a while. Then it straightened out. And *then* . . .

There it was. Birch Cabin. Marked on the map.

"The map makes it clear that this is the path we want," Zack said. He jabbed the map with his finger. "The left one. Come on." He gave Jim a thump on the back. "Let's go."

"Oh, man," Jim said as the two boys began to walk quickly down the path, side by side. "Way to read a map. That was *awesome*. So, now there's something I have to ask."

"What?" asked Zack.

"You're not an alien, are you?"

Chapter Two

Now that Zack and Jim knew where they were going, it didn't take very long to reach the cabin. Just like it showed on the map, the path zigzagged back and forth, winding its way through the trees. *Like a ski slalom,* thought Zack. Then the path straightened just as the guys came to a clearing, and in the clearing was the cabin.

"We made it!" Jim cried. "Birch Cabin. Home sweet home. Cool!"

Zack liked Birch Cabin right away, though it didn't look anything like what he'd pictured in his mind. The word "cabin" made him think of log cabins. He'd expected a sturdy building with round logs for walls.

Instead, Birch Cabin looked more like something that had quietly grown up out of the soft, mossy ground all by itself and was quietly sinking back in. A set of rickety wooden steps led up to a screen door. The whole upper half of the cabin was windows, but they didn't have glass in them. They had screens. Through them, Zack heard a loud burst of laughter. It sounded like a lot of the guys had already made it to the cabin.

Zack suddenly felt hesitant. *What if everybody else has been at camp before?* he thought.

What if I'm the only new guy? He squared his shoulders. *Get over it. Everybody's new once.*

He felt a *whoosh* of air as Jim dashed by him up the steps and pulled the door open. "Come on, Zack!" he cried. "What're you waiting for?"

Not a thing! Zack thought. He sprinted up the steps, through the old screen door, and into the cabin.

Whoa! On the outside, Birch Cabin looked peaceful. Inside, it did not look peaceful at all. Inside, the cabin looked like Zack's room after having been hit by a tornado, multiplied by a thousand. *Impressive mess,* thought Zack.

The campers' trunks looked like they'd exploded open. Shoes, pajamas, T-shirts, comic books, and socks littered the floor, and swim trunks, backpacks, and towels dangled from hooks under the windows. Rows of bunk beds lined the cabin's four walls. Some beds were haphazardly made with tangled-up sheets and blankets, so they looked like they'd already been slept in for a week.

Zack's new cabin mates were sitting on the floor or lounging on their bunks and watching while one kid sorted through the biggest pile of snacks that Zack had ever seen. When the kids saw Zack, they stopped and stared.

Zack swallowed what felt like a huge rock stuck in his throat. Maybe everybody was new *once*. But that one time was pretty hard. *So, this is my second challenge,* Zack thought. *The New Guy Challenge. It's tougher than the one with the map!*

"Hey," he managed to croak.

"Hey," the guy closest to him said right back. He had straight black hair and friendly, dark brown eyes. "I'm Yasu."

"Zack," Zack said.

"Who's that behind you?"

"It's me!" Jim said. He popped out from behind Zack.

"Hey, Jimmy!" Yasu cried. He jumped to his feet and thumped Jim on the shoulder. "I was wondering when you'd show up! How're you doing?"

"Great," Jim said, "but I'm *Jim* now."

"Okay, *Jim*," said Yasu. "You know everybody except the newbies, Kareem and Sean and Vik, right?"

"Sure," Jim nodded. He gave a wave. "Hey, guys. This is Zack. He's new too. Our trail was wicked hard, but Zack totally aced the map challenge."

"*We* totally aced the map challenge," Zack said, grinning at Jim.

"Nice," Yasu said. He turned to the other guys. "Okay, everybody, you know the drill. Sound off."

One by one, the other guys in the cabin rattled off their names. Zack did his best to keep up and think of ways to remember who was who. Sean wore a Red Sox cap. Vik had a tennis racket under his bunk. Kareem had a Camp Wolf Trail T-shirt on that looked really, really old and he was holding a bag of cookies in his hands. Zee had braces, and Yasu was wearing swim trunks, and Nate had a pencil and pad stuck in his back pocket.

"Checking supplies? Excellent," Jim said, when the introductions were over. He brushed past Zack to get closer to the snack pile. "Got anything good?"

"Yeah, a really good haul this year," said Nate.

"I've got Critter Crunch," Zack spoke up. He'd never met *anybody* who didn't love Critter Crunch.

"Regular or peanut?" Nate asked. Fast, like it was a quiz or something.

"Both. Two bags of each," Zack said.

Nate smiled and nodded slowly. "Niiiiice."

"Also, my stepdad's chocolate chip cookies," Zack said. "Best in the universe."

"No way," Kareem, one of the new guys, piped up. "They cannot possibly be as good as the ones I brought. They're my grandma's secret recipe."

"Only one way to settle it," said Zee. "Get over here, Zack. I hereby declare the first ever

Camp Wolf Trail cookie throw-down."

"Okay!" cheered all the guys.

Almost before Zack realized what had happened, he was sitting on the floor and everyone was eating chocolate chip cookies and voting for their favorite.

When the votes were counted, it was an even split: Half of Birch Cabin voted for Kareem's cookies. The other half voted for Zack's.

"We need a tie-breaker," Jim declared.

At exactly that minute, the door to Birch Cabin opened.

"Erik!" all the old campers yelled.

"Hey," the newcomer said. He walked into the cabin and tossed his pack onto a bunk. It bounced once, then stayed put, right in the middle.

Nice work, Zack thought. Erik was definitely somebody who knew the ropes.

"So, what's going on?" Erik asked.

"Cookie throw-down," Yasu explained.

"First ever. Between Kareem's chocolate chip cookies and Zack's." He pointed first to Kareem and then Zack. "They're new this year, and so are Sean and Vik over there."

"Hi," Erik said. "So, whose idea was the throw-down? I'll bet it was yours, Zee."

"Yeah," Zee said.

"I'll tell you a secret," Erik said to Zack. "Watch out for Zee. He's always cooking up crazy ideas."

"Put a sock in it," Zee said. "You're spoiling all the fun. Now I can't play any practical jokes on the new guys."

But Zack could see that Zee was smiling.

"So, which cookie is which?" Erik asked. He picked up one of each and held them up, sort of like he was getting ready to conduct a science experiment. "Wait a minute. Don't tell me."

"Right," Kareem nodded. "That way, it's fairer. We need you to break the tie."

Erik closed his eyes. Then, very slowly, he

took a bite of the cookie in his left hand. He chewed the bite, then swallowed. Then he did the exact same thing with the cookie in his right hand. He repeated the steps until only one bite of each cookie was left.

Zack sneaked a sideways glance at Kareem. He didn't look like the kind of kid who'd get bent out of shape for losing a cookie throw-down, but then, who knew? Some kids at school got mad about *any* loss; Zack could only hope kids at camp were different.

Erik opened his eyes, and everyone leaned closer, waiting.

"The winner is . . ." Erik said and then he shrugged. "Both kinds. They're both so good, I can't decide. I hereby officially declare them both to be the champions of the first ever Camp Wolf Trail cookie throw-down."

"That's so cool!" Jim laughed. "No one wins, no one loses. That makes Kareem and Zack sort of like snack co-captains, or something."

"Way to go, Kareem," Zack said. He

stood and held his hand up to Kareem for a high five. "I gotta admit, I liked your grandma's cookies."

"I liked your stepdad's too," Kareem said as he high-fived Zack. He went on proudly, "And by the way, my grandma invented the recipe. *I* made the cookies."

"There *is* one problem," piped up Sean, one of the new kids. "The cookies are almost gone."

"Don't worry," Zack said. "I'll write to my stepdad and ask him to send some more."

"You do that," Zee said with a smile. "Tell him to address the package to *me*."

"Sure," laughed Zack.

"Go jump in a lake, Zee," joked Nate.

"Hey, good idea," said Erik. "About jumping in the lake, I mean. Let's go get our swim tests over with. Then we can do splash fights at O'Mannitt's Cove. Whaddayuh say?"

"I say, last one in is a rotten egg!" hollered Yasu. He leapt up and, without even bothering to change into their swim trunks, all the Birch Cabiners followed him, stampeding to the lake, shouting and howling like wolves.

AAAAhhh-ROOO!

Zack howled loudest of all.

Late that night, Zack snuggled into his bunk. It was the upper bunk, above Jim's. Zack could hear the cabin counselor, Carlos, snoring a little, and the other guys breathing all around him. Now that he was in bed, Zack was discovering one of the best things about Birch Cabin: It was almost like being outside. You could look out the screen windows from every single bed. Zack had a perfect view of the stars. There were more stars than he ever saw at home in the city at night—*so* many he knew he could never count them all.

It did feel a little weird not to be sleeping in his very own bed. But Zack had his copy of *The Outdoor Adventure Guide* underneath his pillow, safe and sound, just as he always did at home.

All in all, Zack thought this *might* have been one of the very best days of his whole life. He knew that for the *rest* of his life, he'd never forget his first plunge into Evergreen Lake. Down, down he'd slid into the silky water, feeling slippery as a fish, and then he'd burst back up into the sunshine that was blindingly bright and hot.

He'd also never forget his first splash fights at O'Mannitt's Cove, a little inlet near the dock, where the water was so cold it took his breath away. He'd always remember his first camp dinner, too, which had been a cookout down by the lake where the campers roasted hot dogs over the fire.

Slowly, Zack closed his eyes.

"Hey," the new kid named Vik said out loud to whomever else was awake. "I just figured out why it's called O'Mannitt's Cove."

"Why?" asked someone, sounding half asleep. "This better be good."

"Because," said Vik, "when you jump in O'Mannitt's Cove, all you can say is, "Oh, man! It's COLD!"

"Argh," everyone groaned, and Zee heaved his pillow at Vik.

Zack grinned. Yeah, no question. This *was* the very best day of his whole life—so far.

Chapter Three

The next morning, Zack woke up so excited and sat up so fast that . . .

Clunk!

The Outdoor Adventure Guide slid out from under his pillow and tumbled onto the floor next to Jim's bunk.

"Who? What? Where?" Jim said, as he bolted upright. He stared around, wildly. His hair stuck out all to one side, as if he'd slept in a stiff breeze. His eyes were open. But Zack was pretty sure his new friend wasn't really awake yet.

"It's nothing," Zack said. He slid out of

his top bunk to pick up the book. "Sorry."

Jim blinked, then rubbed his eyes. He looked more awake now. "Oh, wow," Jim exclaimed. "Is that what I think it is? *The Outdoor Adventure Guide*? That is the best book ever. I put it on my birthday list this year. I really hope I get one."

"*Shh!* Keep it down, you guys," a pillow-muffled voice said. "I'm asleep, for Pete's sakes."

Another voice said, "What's going on?" Zack looked up to see Erik standing behind him. Erik was yawning, but his eyes were bright. He nodded at the book. "What's that?"

"Only the coolest book in the entire universe," Jim answered before Zack could. "Zack brought it. It's *The Outdoor Adventure Guide.*"

Erik hunkered down beside the bunk. "What are we, in school? I come to camp to get away from books," he said. "What's so cool about this one?"

"It shows you how to do pretty much everything," Zack explained. "Like, see, right here . . ." Zack opened the book. He turned the pages quickly. "It shows how you can make a shelter if you don't have a tent."

Erik scratched his left ear. "I already know how to do that," he said. "Everybody around here does. We never use tents for any of the wilderness treks."

"Well, then, how about this page? Check this out," Jim cut in. He reached around Zack to turn the pages himself. "This shows you how to build a fire without any matches."

Erik scratched his right ear. "We all know how to do that too," he said finally. "So far, all the stuff in that book sounds just like what we do at camp. Why would you want to *read* about stuff you can actually *do*?"

Zack opened his mouth. Then he closed it again. How could he make Erik understand that because he'd always lived in a city, reading *The Outdoor Adventure Guide* was the closest Zack thought he'd ever get to camp? *I can't,* he realized. Somehow, he would have to find a way to *show* Erik that *The Outdoor Adventure Guide* was great, even if you'd been going to camp your whole life.

"Rise and shine, Birch Cabin," Carlos called from outside the door. Zack could hear the clanging of the famous Camp Wolf Trail bell echoing through the woods. Carlos went on, "I can smell the bacon cooking already, and you know what that means!"

"BREAKFASSST!" Erik cheered. He raised both fists in the air and seemed to forget all about Zack's book.

Quickly, Zack stuffed *The Outdoor Adventure Guide* back underneath his pillow and rushed to get dressed. Half the guys had slept in their clothes and were already careening out the door.

"Get a move on, Zack!" hollered Yasu, taking the steps in one leap. "Follow me to the dining hall."

Great green globs of greasy grimy gopher guts . . .

Zack grinned and sang along with the rest of the crowd. The dining hall was the wildest, loudest, and most fun place he'd ever eaten in. Sixty hungry campers squeezed onto long benches along the tables, shouting to friends, pounding rhythms on the shaky tabletops, wolfing down fruit and pancakes, and singing songs at the top of their voices.

"YO, YO, YO, CAMP!" thundered P. L., the camp director, who was tall and skinny with close-cropped white hair. He *had* to thunder to make himself heard over the ruckus.

Immediately, everyone stopped talking, and shouted back together, "YO, YO, YO, P. L.!"

Drop-dead silence followed, and P. L. smiled. "WELLLLLLLCOME TO CAMP, MY FRIENDS!"

"YAHOOO!" the campers answered. Zack thought the whoops and shouts and clapping would blow the roof off the dining hall.

While they ate breakfast, counselors made announcements. Some were silly and funny, like the counselor who spoke pig latin, and said, "Ix-nay on aziness-lay." Other announcements were about the schedule for the day and the jobs for each cluster.

"What's a cluster?" Zack asked Zee.

"It's the group you do your camp jobs with and hike with, and it's also your group on theme days," said Zee. "It's made up of kids of different ages."

"This year, every cluster is going to be named after a knock-knock joke," said Jim. "Like, 'Dwayne the Bathtub, I'm Dwowning.' I saw the list posted, and you, Erik, Kareem, Sean, and I are in a cluster called 'Orange You Glad I Didn't Say Banana?' Vik, Nate, Zee, and Yasu are in 'Isabel Necessary On A Bike?'"

"Every cluster makes up a chant," added Yasu, "and a signature move." He rubbed his stomach and patted his head at the same time.

"Nice," said Sean.

Break*fast* was *fast*. It was nearly over when another voice boomed, "Good morning, Camp Wolf Trail."

"Morning, Skeeter!" the campers boomed back.

Zack looked up from the plate of pancakes and bacon he was powering down to see Skeeter Malone, the cook, standing at the entrance to the dining hall.

To Zack's way of thinking, Skeeter looked just like a cook at camp was *supposed* to look. He was solid. Not fat, just sturdy. His cheeks were shiny as red apples. There was very definitely a twinkle in his sharp brown eyes. He was wearing a denim chef's coat, black-and-white checked chef's pants, and a red bandanna tied around his head. On his feet, Skeeter sported a pair of yellow plastic clogs. At his side was a droopy-eared hound, who wagged his whole body, not just his tail, in happy excitement, and smiled a wide, doggy smile.

"Camp dog Cookie here and I let you cook your own dinners at the cookout last night, but this morning, we want to introduce ourselves to you new campers and to say, 'welcome back' to all of you who've been here before," Skeeter went on. He reached down and gave the dog a pat on the head. "Don't we, boy?"

"Woof!" Cookie said. Then he threw his head back and howled. "ARROOOO!" Everybody in the cafeteria laughed and howled back.

"By the way, new guys," Skeeter continued, "don't believe everything the old campers tell you. They were new guys themselves, not so very long ago.

"But now for the two most important

things of all: Don't feed Cookie, no matter how hard he begs. And never forget the number one rule of eating pancakes."

Zack froze. His mouth was full of pancakes and his fork hung in midair, halfway to his mouth, piled high with another mouthful of the best pancakes he'd ever tasted.

"NO PUDDLING!"

Zack set his fork down with a *splunch*. *No puddling?* What on earth was *that* supposed to mean?

"It means," Skeeter went on, just as if he'd read Zack's mind, "pour on all the maple syrup you like, but make sure you eat it all. I don't want to spot leftover syrup on anybody's plate, lying there in . . ."

"Oh, in a *PUDDLE!*" Zack exclaimed, louder than he meant to. "No puddling! I get it!"

A couple of guys Zack didn't know laughed and cheered for him.

Skeeter beamed, and Cookie took off loping toward Zack as fast as his legs could move, darting between campers' feet until he reached Zack. Zack petted him and scratched him behind his ears. Cookie looked up at him lovingly. Zack wasn't surprised; dogs *always* loved him.

"Hey, new kid! Welcome," said Skeeter. "What cluster are you in, son?"

"Orange You Glad I Didn't Say Banana?" Zack said.

Skeeter put his hands on his hips. He looked Zack up and down. "Okay, Mr. Orange-You-Glad, listen up," the cook said. "I'm going to offer you the deal of a lifetime. You can choose whether your cluster has its turn at breakfast clean-up duty first or last. What do you say?"

"Uh, we . . ." Zack didn't know what to choose.

Erik took charge. "Huddle up, everybody," he said. He gestured for all the Orange-You-Glads in Birch to gather and put their heads together.

"I say . . ." Erik began.

"Hey, wait a minute," Sean interrupted. "Zack got us this break. He should go first."

There was a tense silence that lasted one heartbeat. Zack could tell that Erik was used to speaking out, and all the other guys expected him to as well.

But Erik said, "Sean's right. Zack should go first. Sorry."

"So, Zack," Jim said. "What do you think?"

"I think, let's do clean-up duty right away," Zack said. "Get it over with. That way, we'll be done. Plus, with the no puddling rule, the dishes won't be too gross."

"Good point," Kareem said with a laugh. "I second Zack's vote."

"Me too," Jim agreed.

"Anybody *not* want to go right away, raise your hand," Erik commanded.

Nobody moved a muscle.

"Okay," Erik said. "We have a plan." He leaned back and clapped his hands, just like a quarterback. "Break!"

"So, what'll it be?" Skeeter asked.

Erik opened his mouth. Then he shut it and looked across the table at Zack.

"We'll take *first* duty," Zack answered.

"Excellent." Skeeter grinned. "C'mon, Cookie. Let's go rustle up some aprons for our new best friends, the Orange-You-Glads."

"Woof," Cookie barked agreeably, and after a quick look back at Zack, he followed Skeeter to the kitchen.

Never in a million years would Zack have guessed that washing an Everest-high mountain of sticky dishes could be so much *fun.*

"Where the moon hits your eye like a big pizza pie, that's Camp Wolf Trap," sang Kareem, and pretty soon everyone joined in, yodeling and

hooting and singing the crazy lyrics in fake opera voices. Zack soon saw that Kareem knew *all* the words to *every* camp song, having learned them from his dad and his older brother because both of them used to come to camp. And Jim was a whiz at making up new, funny lyrics to the old tunes.

The Birch Cabiners had met up at the giant metal sinks with the older campers from Spruce Cabin who were also Orange-You-Glads. At first, Zack felt a little self-conscious around the older campers, who seemed so grown-up and confident. But cool as the older guys seemed, they still took time to welcome the newbies to camp and give them tips and advice.

"Newbies!" an older camper named Ibrahima yelled. "All eyes on me. Sponge Clinic." Ibrahima held up four sponges. "No corners cut off means it's a sponge to use on dishes and cups. One corner cut off means use it to wipe off tables and counters. Two corners cut off means use it to scrub greasy, sticky pots and pans. Three corners cut off means it's totally gross. Throw it away fast. Got it?"

Another camper from Spruce Cabin, named Foley, showed the newbies how plastic cups were stacked in a teetery pyramid to dry and dishes were lined up in drying racks.

But in between—and even *during*—dishwashing lessons, kids laughed and blew suds off their soapy arms at each other and drummed out wild rhythms by beating spoons on the bottoms of pots. The Orange-You-Glads also decided that their signature move would be a smooth moonwalk, and their chant would go to the tune of "La Cucaracha":

> *Oh, buddy, Arennn-tcha?*
> *Oh, buddy, Arennn-tcha?*
> *Glad I didn't say bah-nahn-uh!*

When the dishes were done, the Birch Cabin Orange-You-Glads moonwalked their way back through the woods, singing their chant over and over again.

Chapter Four

"I can't find a footprint!" Zee wailed. "I can't even find a *toe* print, for cryin' out loud, and we've been out here for *hours*. What is this, the forest of the flying monkeys?"

It was some time later, after lunch, and all the Birch Cabiners and their counselor, Carlos, were on a tracking expedition, looking for animal tracks in the woods.

Searching for animal tracks was something Zack had always wanted to try. The chapter on tracking in *The Outdoor Adventure Guide* was one of his favorites. He'd tried tracking in the park near his house, but all he ever found were dog tracks. Here he was at last, looking for real wild animal tracks.

"You have to look *closely*," Zack said.

And you have to be patient, he thought. But even Zack had to admit he was starting to get a little discouraged as the afternoon wore on. He hadn't found any tracks either. Nobody had. And Zee was right. It *did* feel like they'd been out in the woods for hours, going around in circles, finding nothing.

So, try harder, Zack said to himself. He hunkered down, trying to get as close to the ground as possible.

"I've *been* looking closely," Erik grumbled. He squatted down beside Zack. "If I look any closer, I'll do a face-plant in the dirt!"

Zack straightened up so quickly that Erik toppled over backward onto the seat of his pants in surprise.

"That's it!" Zack said. "Erik, you're brilliant!"

"Well, duh." Erik grinned as Zack held out a hand and pulled him to his feet. "Everybody knows that. So, um, what did I do that was so smart this time?"

"You said the magic word: dirt," Zack said.

"I can use the word *dirt* in a sentence too," Nate spoke up. "'Erik has dirt all over his rear.'"

Everyone, including Erik, laughed as he dusted himself off.

"What's so great about dirt?" Sean asked.

"Dirt is why we haven't been able to find any tracks," Zack explained. "Dirt's too hard. What we want is some nice, soft *mud*. And I bet I know right where we can find some."

"Me too!" shouted Jim, Zee, and Yasu in unison. And they all took off running.

"Down by the lake, right?" said Nate.

"Right! I saw some great mud in O'Mannitt's Cove," said Zack.

"Follow me," hollered Yasu, who liked to be first.

Like a herd of wild horses, the boys charged through the woods and ran down toward the shore of O'Mannitt's Cove.

"O-kaaay," Zack said, surveying the cool, wet mud on the banks that led to the water. "*This* is more like it."

"Remember not to go into the water, guys," Carlos called out.

"We don't even have to go all the way to the water," Zack called back. "The mud is perfect right here."

Now, all I have to do is find something, he thought.

He crouched down. Any lower, and he'd be crawling on his hands and knees.

"Remind me what we're looking for again?" asked Kareem.

"Anything, really," Zack replied. "Anything that looks like a footprint, I mean."

"But not one of ours," Erik put in.

Zack looked over at Erik. "Duh," he said, just like Erik had earlier. The two guys grinned at each other.

Zack continued his search. He bent low, his eyes fixed on the ground. Then he zigzagged back and forth. Slowly but surely, Zack got closer and closer to a big clump of bushes near the water's edge. Zack was on his fifth "zig" when something caught his eye. Tracks! Fine, clear animal tracks that looked like fossils in the mud and led down to the water.

"Hey, you guys!" Zack yelled. "Over here!"

Zack dropped to his hands and knees in the mud as the rest of the guys sprinted over. They peered over Zack's shoulder.

Jim gave a low whistle. "Wow!" he said. "There are so many prints."

"It has to be a whole family of something, right, Zack?" asked Nate.

Zack studied what he'd found. There was one big set of prints and seven little ones.

"You know," he said. "I think so."

"Cool," Vik said. "But a family of *what*?"

"Hey, wait a minute," Zee suddenly spoke up. "Isn't this where that kid from Pine Cabin saw skunks last year?"

"Very funny, Zee," said Yasu. "Is that one of your jokes?"

"Yeah, but *skunks*?" bleated Kareem.

"Take it easy," said Zack. "These can't be skunk tracks."

"How can you be so sure?" Erik asked.

"Skunks have five toes," Zack said. "These tracks only have four toes, so whatever these guys are, they're definitely not skunks."

"How do you know that?" Erik asked. "Wait a minute. Don't tell me. It's in that book of yours, right?"

"Right," Zack said. "In the chapter about tracking."

"You and that book," laughed Erik.

"Um, guys?" Carlos said. His voice sounded funny. Like Zack's mom's voice did whenever she was worried about something but trying hard not to show it. Carlos pointed. "Look."

Everybody turned and looked. Standing between the boys and the lake was the first official wild animal Zack had ever seen. It had a pointed snout and a bushy tail. It was black all over, except for the thin, white stripe running down between its bright, black eyes and a tuft of white at the top of its head, like a furry white hat. Down its back ran two white stripes.

"Hey, that's a *skunk!*" Zack cried. In his surprise, his voice came out loud. Very loud.

The skunk made a funny hissing sound. It turned around, lifted its tail, and . . .

"Everybody run!" Carlos shouted.

The boys took off, stumbling into one another, tripping over their own feet, yelling, "SKUNNNNKKK!" and running away from the skunk and away from the lake as fast as their legs could carry them. They hadn't run more than a few yards before the worst smell— rank, reeking, and pungent—swallowed them up. The air was so thick with the horrible odor that Zack thought he could almost *see* the smell weighing down the breeze from the lake, surrounding the boys in a great cloud of stink, so strong it was suffocating.

"Oh, man, this is *gross*!" Erik choked.

"No talking," Carlos gasped out. "Get away from the lake. Run to the flagpole. Go, go, go!"

Zack's eyes watered. Branches *whacked* against his legs and arms no matter what path he took. He could hear the other guys panting as they ran hard. That's when Zack realized he was panting, too, sucking huge gulps of air in and out of his mouth. Anything to avoid using his nose, which was runny. Anything to avoid having to smell the *smell*, which clung on, no matter how far or fast he ran.

Zack threw himself onto the ground near the rest of the boys, and they gathered around the flagpole. His chest heaved up and down. Some of the boys stayed standing, bent over, sucking in air, coughing, spitting, their hands braced on their knees.

"Nice—work—genius," Erik choked out, glaring at Zack, making it clear he meant the exact opposite of what he'd said. But he *did* mean it when he said, "This stinking mess is your fault. You and your *book*."

Zack swallowed and tried to speak, but before he could, Yasu spoke up.

"Back off, Erik," said Yasu.

"Yeah, take it easy," said Jim. "I kind of think the skunk-scapade's funny. Shoot, I've smelled worse than this all on my own."

Just then, Skeeter and Cookie appeared. "What in the *world*?" Skeeter exclaimed.

"Aaaoooooeee," Cookie gave an agonized howl.

"Whew! You said it, boy," Skeeter agreed. "I guess I don't need to ask what happened to you guys."

"Can you help?" asked Carlos.

"I can," said Skeeter. "Though you might not like the solution any more than you like the problem."

"*Nothing* could be worse than this," said Zee.

"Okay, then," said Skeeter. "Everybody follow me."

Zack lagged way behind as Skeeter led the smelly pack of boys, still coughing and rubbing their eyes, behind the dining hall, where there was an old metal washtub that looked like a horse's water trough. Right next to it, balanced on two sawhorses, was a wooden door that Skeeter used as an outdoor table for chopping vegetables and husking corn.

By the time Zack joined the others, Skeeter

had lined up a row of giant cans of tomato juice on the door.

"Okay, everybody," Skeeter said. "In the washtub, one at a time, clothes and all. You're going to have the pleasure of a tomato juice bath."

"Aw, *man*," griped Nate.

Kareem shook his head sadly as he looked down at his shirt. "My dad wore this shirt when he was a camper here, and my brother did, too," he said. "And now it'll probably be wrecked. For good."

"I'm sorry," Zack said. "Really, everybody, I'm sorry."

But no one acknowledged his apology.

"I don't even *drink* tomato juice," Zee was complaining. "Now I'm going be drowned in it."

"I need a volunteer to open these cans," said Skeeter, ignoring all the whining.

"Zack volunteers," Erik said sharply. He didn't look at Zack. But that didn't matter:

Zack wouldn't have been able to look him in the eye anyway. "Zack's the one who found the skunk."

"Okay, Zack," said Skeeter. "Grab the can opener and start cranking." Then Skeeter ordered, "First guy into the tub!"

"I'll go!" said Jim.

Zack gritted his teeth. He set the can opener against the rim of the tomato juice can and cranked with all his might. When the cap was open, Skeeter poured the juice over Jim's head. *Glug, glug, glug.* Red, goopy juice ran down Jim's face, over and under his T-shirt, and down his arms.

"Yeee-owww! That's cold," said Jim. He rubbed the tomato juice all over him, scrubbing his armpits as if he were taking a shower in soapy water, and energetically shampooing his hair.

Some of the boys laughed at Jim's goofy showering. Then, grudgingly, one by one the Birch Cabiners stepped into the tub and scrubbed the skunk smell off and the tomato juice smell on.

As they did, Skeeter glanced over at Zack and grinned. "You've had quite an afternoon, haven't you, son?" he said kindly. "And this is only your first full day at camp. Looks like you're going to have a wild summer."

Zack grinned back, but his grin was weak and watery. He couldn't forget what Erik had said. The skunk catastrophe *was* Zack's fault. *The Outdoor Adventure Guide* had let him down, and then he had let his buddies down. Talk about a stinking mess!

Zack stayed at Skeeter's side, opening every last can of tomato juice in the Camp Wolf Trail kitchen. Then, finally, after everybody else was through and Skeeter had left to get dinner ready, Zack took his turn. He scrubbed off the skunk smell, but even after his tomato juice bath, Zack still felt as low-down as a skunk.

Chapter Five

Zack trudged back to Birch Cabin, trying his best to ignore all the sounds of the bustling camp around him. If he didn't look at anything or anybody, maybe nobody would look at him. Right at that moment, what Zack wanted more than anything in the world was to be The Invisible Man. Instead, he knew he was the sunburn-pinkish, tomato-scented-with-smelly-undertones-of-skunk boy.

Zack's feet felt like lead as he climbed the steps to Birch Cabin and pulled open the screen door. Every single one of his cabin mates was inside Birch Cabin and every single one stared at

Zack. They were peeling off their ruined clothes and piling them in a damp heap in one corner. All except Kareem, that is. He hung his T-shirt out the window. The cabin was suspiciously quiet, as if a conversation had stopped mid-sentence the minute Zack had appeared.

Wham! Zack let the screen door slam shut behind him. Now, Zack's legs felt like they were made of lead. The trip from the door to his bunk seemed to take forever. Zack swung himself up onto his bunk. And that's when it happened. For the second time that day, Zack's copy of *The Outdoor Adventure Guide* slid out from underneath his pillow and fell with a *thunk* to the floor.

Zack stared down at the book. It had been his most valuable possession until about an hour ago. Now, he didn't even want to touch it.

How had it happened? How had the *Guide* let him down?

Slowly, Zack climbed down from his bunk to pick up the book.

"I'd put that thing away and never look at it again if I were you," Erik said. "Reading it is just a waste of time. I think we all proved *that*."

"You can say that again," muttered Kareem.

Erik stood up. "C'mon you guys," he said to everyone but Zack. "Time for dinner. In fact, thanks to our tomato baths, we're almost late. We don't even have time for a real shower or even a quick dunk in the lake to try to get rid of the spaghetti sauce smell."

One by one, Zack's cabin mates followed Erik as he stomped out the door. Zack didn't know whether they all looked mad or not. He was too busy staring at the floor. He couldn't bring himself to look at anyone.

Then he heard Jim say, "Listen, Zack, don't pay any attention to Erik. He'll cool down. And Kareem'll figure out how to rescue his shirt. The rest of the guys are just afraid of being laughed at."

Zack looked up quickly. "And you're not?"

Jim gave an odd little snort. "I'm used to it," he said. "Happens to me all the time. Besides, as I said before, I thought the skunk thing was kind of funny, not tragic."

"Look, Jim, thanks for talking to me when nobody else would," Zack said. "But you and I both know that I screwed up. It's probably better if you don't hang out with me. You should go to dinner with the rest of the guys."

"But . . ." Jim began.

"Jim," Zack said quietly. "Just go."

Jim hesitated for a moment. Then, without

another word, he left the cabin. He closed the screen door quietly behind him.

Zack sat perfectly still. He stared down at *The Outdoor Adventure Guide*. Then, like a hawk swooping down on an unsuspecting mouse, Zack leaned down and snatched up the *Guide*. Feverishly, he leafed through the pages until he found the section about animal tracks.

Zack knew there was an example of a skunk print in the book. He *knew* it. He'd read the chapter on tracking more than once. So, why hadn't he known the print he found in the woods belonged to a skunk?

How had everything gone so terribly wrong?

There! There was the skunk print. Zack leaned over the book until his nose practically bumped the page. Silently, he counted off the number of toes: One, two, three, four, five!

Five toes! He hadn't gotten it wrong after all! So why . . .

All of a sudden, Zack made a strangled

sound. He noticed something he never had before. Near the picture of the skunk footprint was a little icon of a magnifying glass. It meant that there was more to see. *Turn to the appendix to find out more*, it read beside the icon.

Slowly, Zack turned the pages. There it was, way back in the appendix, a second skunk footprint. This one had *four* toes.

Some tracks, like this skunk footprint, can fool you, Zack read. *Skunks really* do *have five toes. But the fifth toe almost never leaves a mark. So, you're more likely to spot a print that looks like this one.*

With a *wham*, Zack closed the book. Then he knelt down and yanked his trunk out from underneath the lower bunk. He opened the lid, tossed the book inside, slammed the lid shut, and shoved the trunk back under the bed—*hard*.

Zack slumped on the floor. He stared straight out into space. Skunk footprints, some with four toes, some with five, danced before his eyes.

He *had* screwed up. *He* had. Not *The*

Outdoor Adventure Guide. The information that could have kept Zack and the rest of Birch Cabin skunk-free was right there inside the book. But Zack had carelessly missed it somehow. And now he and everybody else in Birch Cabin were paying for his carelessness.

Everybody has a perfect right to be mad at me, Zack thought. Word of what had happened would be all over camp by now. Everyone in Birch Cabin was sure to get laughed at. And it was all Zack's fault.

I want to go home, Zack thought. *Back to the city where things are familiar.* Zack didn't want any more adventures. Not if they were going to turn out like this one.

He heard a squeak as the screen door of Birch Cabin opened.

"Hey, Zack," said a quiet voice.

"Hey, Carlos," Zack said.

"Mind if I sit down?"

Zack looked up at his counselor.

"Aren't you afraid I might contaminate

you or something?"

"I think I'll risk it," Carlos said. He sat down on a trunk. "So," Carlos said after a moment, "are you coming to dinner?"

"I don't know," Zack answered.

"Honestly?"

Zack stole a look at the counselor. Carlos had gotten skunk-bombed and tomato-bathed right along with the rest of Birch Cabin. He should be mad at Zack, just like everybody else was. But he didn't look mad, Zack thought. Carlos looked . . . just like he always did. Like he was somebody you could like and trust. Someone you wouldn't want to lie to.

Zack sighed and said again, "I don't know."

Carlos smiled. "Look, Zack," he said. "I know that some things here at camp haven't gone the way you hoped. But other things have been totally awesome! Jim told me about how you hit the map challenge out of the park. And today, you figured out why we weren't finding

any tracks and where to go to look for them."

"Yeah," Zack agreed. "And look how well that turned out."

"You know what the very best thing about being a counselor at Camp Wolf Trail is?" Carlos asked suddenly.

"No. What?" Zack asked, surprised.

"Getting to know the guys in my cabin," Carlos replied. "You learn to spot strengths in people right away, because you don't have all that much time to get to know them. Do you want to know what I see in you?"

Zack shrugged. "I guess so."

"I see a problem-solver. That's a pretty great skill to have. And so I know that you'll figure out a way to solve the problem you're having right now."

"You mean the problem where everybody else in Birch Cabin wishes I was going to camp in a different galaxy?" Zack asked.

"That's the one," Carlos nodded.

Zack sat for a moment, letting Carlos's

words sink in.

"Thanks," Zack said. "Thanks for not telling me I should just get over it."

"No problem," Carlos said. "Truthfully? I don't think anybody just 'gets over' anything. I think you have to *do* something about the things that bother you."

"So, what you want to know," Zack said, "is, what am I going to do about this?"

"Not quite," Carlos said. "What I want is for *you* to know what you're going to do about it."

"Because you think I'm a good problem-solver?"

"Because I *know* you're a good problem solver." Carlos stood up. "You've apologized, but maybe you could stand up and own the mess somehow, if you see what I mean. Anyway, I have to go. I'm starved."

Zack sat up straight. He *did* see what Carlos meant, and he knew who could help him too. "Hey, Carlos," he said, just before the counselor got to the door.

"Yeah?"

"Knock, knock."

"Who's there?"

"Orange."

"Orange, who?"

"Orange you glad there was only one skunk at the lake?"

"Oh," moaned Carlos, holding his forehead as if he were in pain. "That's *terrible*." He grinned. "But, I see what you're doing. You've already figured out that joking is a great way to defuse a bomb and turn a bad situation around. Go for it, buddy. See you at dinner. Good luck!"

Chapter Six

By the time Zack got to the dining hall, the sun was sinking down toward the lake and the rest of camp was already at dinner. P. L. was at one end of the dining hall, talking to a group of counselors. Zack spotted the rest of Birch Cabin sitting together at a table about halfway up the hall.

There was room for him with his cabin mates, but Zack eased into an empty spot near the back of the hall. As he sat down, one of the guys next to him inhaled a deep breath.

"Guess we're having spaghetti for dinner," the boy said. He said it really loud, but he grinned to show that he was only teasing.

This was just the opening Zack was waiting for. Even though he felt his face beginning to turn the color of his recent tomato juice bath, Zack climbed up on top of his table. He flung his arms out wide and sang at the top of his voice to the tune of "Great Green Globs":

Grab a can of
Skeeter's red tomato juice.
Rip it open,
Pour it loose.
Take your baths in
Vats of cold tomato juice.
Watch out for that skunk!
Go, Birch!

The dining hall erupted in wild cheers.

And Cookie, who for some reason seemed to be under the impression that all the fuss was for him, threw back his head and howled happily.

Arooo!

Then Cookie settled himself at Zack's feet, looking up at Zack with adoration. *At least I've got one supporter,* Zack thought, *even if he is only a dog.*

But Zack hadn't even started to eat before Jim scrambled on top of his table and sang to the tune of "On Top of Old Smokey":

> *Us guys in Birch Cabin*
> *Were reeking of skunk*
> *But after our juice baths*
> *We'd taste good for lunch.*

Zack shot Jim a grateful grin as all the kids in the dining hall laughed and shouted, "YO, YO, YO, BIRCH!" Carlos was right: Humor had turned it all around so that Birch Cabin was cool because of the skunk-scapade, as Jim had called it.

Good old Jim, thought Zack. *I knew he'd be crazy enough to help me. You've gotta be crazy to sing in front of everybody on your first full day of camp.*

Then Zack was surprised as Kareem

climbed up on the table next to Jim and sang to the tune of "When the Moon Hits Your Eye Like a Big Pizza Pie":

When the smell hits your nose
Like some ripe toe-may-toes
That's Birch Cabin.

And everyone in the dining hall repeated the last line:

That's Birch Cabin!

P. L. was laughing as hard as everyone else, but he held up his hands to signal for quiet. "Okay, everybody," P. L. said. "Let's keep it down to a dull roar."

When the campers got a bit quieter, P. L. continued: "So, it's clear that Birch Cabin's skunk experience is going to go down in Camp Wolf Trail history as a pretty hilarious goofball mess up. Way to go, Birch Cabiners!"

Zack breathed a sigh of relief when he saw all his fellow cabin mates stand up and cheer and take bows. Yasu raised both fists over his head like a boxing champion, and Zee waved his hands to make everyone cheer longer and louder.

Zack then caught Erik's eye. Erik shrugged and grinned. *Okay,* Zack thought. *I'm forgiven. But being forgiven is just the first step. It's not the same as winning back trust or respect. Somehow, I have to convince the guys I'm not a lame-brain loser. That's not going to be so easy, especially when I don't* trust *myself* anymore.

"Hey, wait up!"

It was after dinner, and Zack was headed through the softly shadowed woods back to Birch Cabin when Jim called out to him. Zack waited while Jim caught up.

"Nice song, buddy," said Jim. He pitched his voice high as he repeated the last lines from Zack's song: *Watch out for that skunk! Go Birch!*

"Your song wasn't too shabby either,"

said Zack. "*Us guys in Birch Cabin, were reeking of skunk . . .*" He and Jim laughed. Then Zack said, "Hey, listen, sorry I acted so lousy before."

"Zack," Jim said. "We're friends. Friends don't stay mad at each other. They get over it."

No, they don't, Zack thought suddenly. He remembered his conversation with Carlos. *Real friends don't stay mad because they do something. And what they do is that they decide that being friends is more important than being mad.*

"Thanks," Zack said.

Jim shrugged. "No big deal. I . . ."

But just then, both Zack and Jim heard a strange sound. *Rustle. Rustle.*

"What was that?" Zack asked. He spun around. He peered through the dusky maze of the tree trunks and the tangle of underbrush, trying to see what was coming. How'd the woods get so dark so fast?

Rustle. Rustle. Crunch.

Zack could hear the sound of bushes being trampled and pushed aside, the sound an animal makes running through the woods to attack.

Rustle. Rustle. Rustle. Crunch. Crunch.

"Zee? Is that you playing a lame joke?" Zack called.

Rustle. Rustle. Crunch. Crunch. Crunch.

The sound was getting closer. And faster. Coming at a dead run. Zack swore that he could hear breathing, now, and it made his blood run cold. He heard a deep panting, *huh, huh, huh,* like whatever it was had been running for a long time.

Huh. Huh. Huh. Crunch. Crunch. CRUNCH.

A figure burst from the bushes in a great rush. It was too dark in the moonless woods to see much, but a huge tongue flopped down over the creature's pointed teeth. Saliva dripped from its mouth.

"Aaaaaooooo!"

The creature threw back its head and gave an unearthly howl. And then it bounded toward the boys, lunging full speed and full force through the air, its glittering eyes fixed on Zack.

Chapter Seven

"It was Cookie," Zack announced.

The campers around the fire circle laughed.

"He came at me so fast, out of the pitch dark, he knocked me down."

"You could have knocked *me* down with a feather, I was so scared," added Jim. "I was sure that we were about to find out why this camp is called *Wolf* Trail."

Everybody cheered. Then somebody started to clap. Pretty soon everyone around the fire circle was clapping and whistling and stomping their feet.

"Cookie, Cookie, Cookie," they chanted.

Cookie, who was sitting next to Zack just as he always did whenever he had a chance, threw back his head and gave a howl. It didn't sound quite so scary to Zack now that he was sitting safely around the crackling fire with everyone. But earlier that night . . .

"All right, all right," P. L. said. He was grinning too as he stood up and motioned for silence. It took a few minutes for everybody to quiet down.

"That is quite a story," P. L. said when order had been restored. "A really great way to start our very first fire circle. I do have a question, though. Why was Cookie chasing you, Zack?"

Zack shrugged. "Dogs love me," he said. "Cookie's crazy about me, and also . . ." Zack stopped. "I didn't mean to!" he burst out.

"Oh, ho! A mystery," P. L. exclaimed. "Didn't mean to what?"

"Feed the dog," admitted Zack sheepishly.

A sympathetic laugh swept around the fire

circle. Firelight lit up all the faces, and sparks flew like fireflies up into the inky night sky. Smoke curled above the fire and made Zack's eyes water, but he moved in closer for the warmth.

"And just how did that happen?" Skeeter asked. "'Cause I know you know the rule against feeding Cookie."

"Well, when I was doing dishes this morning," Zack confessed, "Cookie was next to me, and a piece of leftover bacon fell off one of the plates. I tried to get to it first, but . . ."

"But Cookie was just too fast for him," Jim said. "I saw it all. Man, oh man. I don't think I've *ever* seen a dog slurp up a piece of anything so fast."

"That's my boy," Skeeter said. He gave Cookie a pat on the head. Cookie thumped his tail proudly.

"Ever since then, all day long," Zack picked up the story, "I've been Cookie's new best friend. He thinks I slipped him some bacon, so he'll follow me anywhere. Right, Cookie?"

"Aaaaaoooo!" Cookie howled in complete agreement, and so enthusiastically that everyone had to cheer for him again.

Chapter Eight

"Hey," Zack said. He pointed to the lake. "Those kayakers are going around in circles."

From his seat on a nearby fallen log, Kareem laughed. "Why do you think they call it 'Oddball Championships'?"

It was the next day, and Zack's cluster, the Orange-You-Glads, were on the first leg of their wilderness trek. Other clusters had stayed back at camp for Oddball Championships or had gone on other trips. The Orange-You-Glads were taking their lunch break. The noontime sun was warm on Zack's back and his hummus and pita bread sandwich tasted great, the best he'd ever had. In front of him, the water of Evergreen Lake sparkled. And there were the Oddball Champions, paddling in a circle like they were actually going somewhere.

"How will they tell who wins?" asked Sean.

"Everybody wins," Erik answered, his mouth full of apple. "It's Crazy Cool Racing Day. You paddle as fast as you can until one of the counselors blows the whistle. The only way to *not* win is to stop paddling."

"And nobody ever does that," Jim said. He was sitting next to Zack. "In the first place, if you did, all the guys behind you would crash into you. And in the second place . . ." He waved his sandwich enthusiastically. "It's so much fun that once you start, you just can't stop!"

"Kind of like hiking in the woods," Carlos's voice sounded above their heads. "Okay, guys, we head out in five minutes. Time to finish up lunch."

All the boys finished their sandwiches

quickly and even ate their apple cores. The whole time they were on the wilderness trek, not one piece of trash or leftover food would get left behind to litter the forest. Zack lifted his pack and slipped his arms through the straps so that it lay flat against his back. He loved the feeling of carrying only what he'd need to survive in the woods for two nights and three days: water, his share of the group's collective food and cooking supplies, extra clothes and socks, rain poncho, sleeping bag, and flashlight.

As the boys hiked deeper and deeper into the woods, farther and farther away from camp, Zack's spirits soared. All his life he'd wanted to hike like this, far away from buildings and cars, wires and sidewalks and people. He was glad his cluster was doing the wilderness hike first, though he looked forward to the other trips (and the Oddball Championships *did* look like fun). But tonight, he'd chow down on hot dogs cooked over a cookstove, lie out surrounded by stars, and fall asleep listening to owls hooting and the wind rustling the treetops.

Even though the guys in Birch Cabin were the youngest kids in their cluster, they kept up with the older, longer-legged Orange-You-Glads from Spruce Cabin and their counselors just fine. So far, none of the older guys in the cluster had mentioned the skunk incident— not once. Even the spaghetti sauce jokes were starting to taper off. With any luck, Zack hoped, they were over for good.

"Hey, Erik," Zack suddenly heard Foley

say. "What's your favorite kind of meatball?"

Zack saw Erik's shoulders tense.

I guess the jokes are not *over,* Zack thought. *I have to do something.* Nobody would be teasing Erik if it hadn't been for Zack. "I know what *my* favorite kind of meatball is," Zack spoke up in a loud voice.

"Oh yeah? What kind?" asked Foley.

"Turkey," Zack said.

"Turkey?" said Foley.

"Honestly?" Zack said. "When I looked at you, it was the first word that popped into my mind."

"Gobble, gobble," added Sean.

"I like baloney meatballs," said Jim.

"So *that's* why you're full of baloney most of the time," joked Kareem.

"Oh, man," sighed Sean. "I'm so hungry, even a baloney meatball sounds good to me now."

"How about a nice cold glass of tomato juice with that?" joked Jim.

Foley started to laugh. "You Birch Cabiners are crazy," he said, shaking his head.

Zack couldn't quite see Erik's face, because Erik was ahead of him. But he was pretty sure Erik was okay, because his shoulders were loose and relaxed.

Before lunch, the guys from Birch Cabin and Carlos had hiked at the back of the group, because they were taking turns being Sweep for the leg of the hike from Camp Wolf Trail to the far side of the lake. Sweep was an important position. The Sweep brought up the rear, making sure nobody was left behind. It was a job for a counselor, but the Sweep always welcomed campers to help with the job.

But after lunch, the Birch Cabiners hiked up front and took turns at Point with the counselor there. The boy who was Point went first, following the trail blazes and leading the way for the rest of the Orange-You-Glads.

Now that the Birch Cabiners were in front,

Sean insisted that they try to hike a little ahead of the older boys and put some space between the two groups, so that their group could hike silently.

"If we're quiet, we'll see animals," Sean instructed them in a soft voice. Sean was right. As they hiked, the boys saw squirrels, chipmunks, deer, and birds. They saw footprints of animals that usually came out at night, like raccoons, rabbits, and even a fox.

Zack kept his voice low when he said, "You know, I'm not so sure I like the look of those clouds."

"What are you all of a sudden? The weather man?" Erik asked.

"No, really," Zack said. "I've been keeping my eye on them all afternoon." He pointed. "You can't even see the top of the hill anymore."

Since the lunch break by the lake, the boys had been hiking steadily on a trail that zigzagged up a steep mountainside. Every time they zigged or zagged up, it felt to Zack as if the clouds dropped lower. The air had turned so hot and thick and muggy that the hikers felt like they were slogging through soup.

"Zack's right," Jim said. "I hadn't noticed the clouds before."

"Okay, but so what?" Kareem asked. "The worst that can happen is that it will rain, right? We've all been wet before."

"I don't care about us getting wet," Zack said. "I'm worried about the ground."

"You're worried about the *ground*?" Kareem echoed. His rescued T-shirt, still pinkish from the tomato juice bath, was stained a dark rusty color where it stuck to his back with sweat.

"I just mean that the path is getting. . . well, squishier and slimier and slipperier the higher we climb," Zack said.

To prove his point, he lifted up one foot and stomped down hard. Zack's hiking boot sank down into the muck. When he lifted his foot up again, it made a weird, sucking sound.

"And look up there," he said, pointing to the hillside.

"Wow!" Sean exclaimed. "It sort of looks like somebody took a big bite out of the mountain."

"Yeah," Jim agreed. "More than one. You think the ground is collapsing because it's so wet?"

"I don't know," Zack shrugged.

Since being so sure—and then so *wrong*—about the skunk tracks, Zack wasn't positive about anything. He didn't trust himself. He wouldn't blame anyone else for not trusting him, either.

"Let's keep moving," said Erik. "Maybe the path is drier up ahead." But after the Birch Cabiners had hiked only a short time more, suddenly Erik said, "Whoa!"

He stopped walking so abruptly that Kareem crashed into him. Erik leaned forward, balancing on his toes. He windmilled his arms, desperately trying to keep from taking even one more step.

"Quick!" Jim shouted. Together, he and Kareem grabbed Erik and hauled him backward. All of the Birch Cabiners gathered around.

"What is it?" Carlos called out from behind them. "Why have you guys stopped?"

"Come see," Erik called back.

In front of the hikers was the biggest mud puddle that Zack had ever seen. It covered the path from side to side. Actually, the word *puddle* sounded too simple to really do it justice, Zack thought. It was more like an evil, sucking mud pit, and a deep, slimy, treacherous one at that.

"Holy guacamole," breathed Jim.

Carlos studied the water. The expression on his face was serious. "We're going to have to go straight through it," he said. "I don't want us trying to go around, particularly not on the down slope side. The ground is way too wet, and we'd risk sliding down the mountain."

"But, it's a ginormous puddle of muck, like a bottomless sinkhole!" Kareem protested. "We'll all get soaked up to our knees!"

"Getting wet *can* be dangerous, especially once the sun goes down and it gets cold," said Carlos. "The trouble is, I don't think we have a choice. There's just no room to go around. We have to go straight through." He tucked his pants into his boots. "I'll go first."

By now the older boys in the cluster and their counselors had caught up so that all of the Orange-You-Glads were gathered to watch Carlos wade cautiously into the puddle. Zack could feel the rest of the hikers press in close.

"It's slippery," Carlos reported from about halfway across. He kept walking, slowly, arms outstretched for balance. He lifted up one foot and set it down carefully before picking up the other foot. When he reached the far side of the puddle, Carlos turned around to face the guys.

"It's not too bad," he reported. "The water never went over the top of my boots. So, here's the plan. Birch Cabiners, you come through first. You older guys from Spruce, hang back. Everybody, take it slow."

Carlos was right, Zack thought a couple of minutes later when it was his turn to slog through the mud pit. It *was* slippery underfoot. And it was a weird kind of slippery, like the mud was trying to make him lose his balance by grabbing on to his feet and holding on. Zack kept his gaze focused on Carlos. It was good to have a goal.

"Great job, guys," Carlos said, as Jim, the last Birch Cabiner, finally reached the other side. "Keep going down the trail a little, will you? I don't want us to get all bottled up. There's a curve just ahead. Go around it and then stop. Stick together. I'll stay here to be sure nobody slips and falls in the mud. After they've crossed, I'll send the guys down to you."

"Okay, Carlos," Erik said.

The Birch Cabiners followed the path that curved close to the mountainside, their boots squishy with puddle water and their legs spattered with mud. They had all rounded the curve so that Carlos and the other hikers were no longer in sight, when *CRACK!*

Zack's head jerked upward at the loud, sharp sound. *What was that?*

Crack! Crack! Snap!

"What was that?" Kareem shouted. "What's going on?"

"I think . . ." Zack began.

That was as far as he got. Above Zack's head, he heard a noise that sounded exactly like someone moaning.

"That's not good," Sean said. "That *cannot* be good."

"But what *is* it?" Jim asked. "Where's it coming from?"

Frantically, the hikers looked in every direction, trying to figure out where the sound was coming from. Beneath Zack's hiking boots, he felt the path begin to shake.

Boom. Boom! Rumble! BOOM!

"It's coming from behind us!" Jim shouted.

"Let's run back to Carlos!" Zack yelled.

He raced back toward the mud puddle.

The other guys were right behind him. All around them, the whole world was going wild. The earth shivered and shook beneath their feet. Rocks and plants came bouncing down the hillside. Zack dodged a huge rock and kept on going. He skidded around the bend in the path and practically collided with Ibrahima, one of the guys from Spruce Cabin, who was running toward him down the path.

"Follow me!" Ibrahima shouted as he passed Zack and the other boys without stopping. "Come on."

But Zack and the other Birch Cabiners hesitated. They could see Carlos wading into the puddle to help Foley, who had slipped and fallen.

Then, *Crrraaaack!*

Above the mud puddle, the hillside split apart. Before Zack's horrified gaze, a great tongue of mud and rocks and plants thundered straight down in a nightmarish cascade, a lava

flow of mud and earth, rocks, boulders, and uprooted trees.

"Look out!" Zack shouted.

But there was no way that anyone could hear him. Zack couldn't even hear himself! The great roar of the landslide seemed to eat up every other sound as the huge, wet mountain of earth swallowed the path, creating a giant, impassable wall that divided the Birch Cabiners from Carlos and the other counselors and all the older boys, except Ibrahima.

Chapter Nine

"CARLOS!" Zack shouted.

He staggered forward. Zack could feel Jim tugging on his arm. He turned toward him.

Jim's eyes were as big as moons. His lips were moving, but Zack couldn't understand a word. Zack tried to pull away, desperate to get to Carlos, but Jim held on tight. He shook his head back and forth from side to side, mouthing, "You can't get to Carlos. Stay back."

And then, as suddenly as it had started, the landslide stopped. Everything was very, very quiet. Zack and Jim stared at one another. They were both afraid to move a muscle.

"Do you think it's over?" Jim whispered.

Slowly, as if any sudden movement might trigger another slide, Zack nodded. "I sure hope so."

"Guys," Zack heard a voice behind him gasp. He and Jim spun around.

Erik was clambering to his feet. Sean and Kareem were helping him up. They were muddy and wet, but they were all right.

"We're cut off," Jim began. "Carlos and everybody else but Ibrahima is on the other side of the landslide. They can't hear us or get to us. We . . ."

"Where's Ibrahima?" Erik choked out.

Ibrahima!

The Birch Cabiners ran down the rock-littered path and around the curve. Ibrahima was lying on his side in a muddy twist of the path. He was spattered with wet mud, and he wasn't moving. He *couldn't* move. One leg was pinned under a heavy, cruel-looking tree trunk, and he was entangled in a web of twisted branches that held him fast.

Zack threw himself down at Ibrahima's side while the other Birch Cabiners pulled the tree away. "Ibrahima!" Zack said.

Ibrahima moaned. He opened his eyes, then closed them again, as if he were drifting in and out of being awake.

"Come on, you guys," said Zack. "Help me lift the trunk off his leg."

Frantically, all the boys worked to free Ibrahima from the muddy earth and fallen tree. Once his legs were uncovered, they pulled him forward as gently as they could.

Zack collapsed onto the path. He was breathing hard.

"We have to get some help. Help!" Sean shouted. He turned back toward the slide. "Can anybody hear us? Help. Help. HELP!"

Zack lifted his head to listen. He thought he heard a faint sound, as if somebody was trying to answer but was too far away for the words to be heard or to make any sense at all.

Zack got to his feet as the truth began to sink in.

"Jim's right," he said. "We're on our own."

"But we can't be on our own," Kareem protested. "That's not supposed to happen."

"I don't see anybody else, do you?" Erik snapped.

"Guys," Jim said. "Chill."

"What do you mean *chill*?" Kareem said. "I can't chill! I don't want us to be on our own!"

"Nobody wants that," Jim said.

"So, what are we going to do?" Sean asked. He looked at Erik.

"I don't know," Erik said. "Maybe we should just wait here until someone comes to find us."

"No," Zack shook his head. "We can't do that. It'll take too long. Ibrahima needs help."

"We all do," said Sean. "Remember what Carlos said? It'll get cold at night. And we're all muddy and wet, especially Ibrahima."

"So, how are we supposed to move him?"

Erik asked. "We can't just pick him up. And we don't have a stretcher or anything."

"No," Zack said. The word came out slowly, even though his mind was working in hyper-drive.

Come on, Zack, think! he told himself. Carlos had called him a good problem-solver. It was time to prove him right. What would *The Outdoor Adventure Guide* advise? Zack thought hard, and the memory of an illustration from the *Guide* swam into his head. The illustration showed a sledge made of tree branches that could be used to drag heavy weights . . .

"Could we drag him, maybe?" Zack said, as if he were thinking out loud. "What if we put him on something and pulled him?"

"Drag him?" Sean asked. "On what?"

"I don't know," said Zack. "Branches? Or does anybody have a tarp?"

"I do," said Erik. He pulled a thick canvas tarp out of his backpack. "Carlos asked me to pack it in case of rain."

"That's it then," said Jim.

It took about five minutes of huffing and puffing, but finally the tarp was on the path and Ibrahima was on the tarp. He'd groaned once or twice and winced with pain as the guys moved him, even though they'd moved him as gently as they could. Now the stranded hikers stood around the tarp, sucking in air and staring down at Ibrahima, who lay still, with his eyes closed, breathing hard.

Now that they were actually putting his plan into action, Zack was starting to have doubts. Just getting Ibrahima onto the tarp had been hard. Were the five of them really strong enough to pull him all the way back to safety? They didn't even know how far away from safety they were.

Zack had been wrong about the skunk. If he was wrong about this, the consequences were much more serious—maybe even life and death.

"Okay," Erik said. "So, what's the plan?"

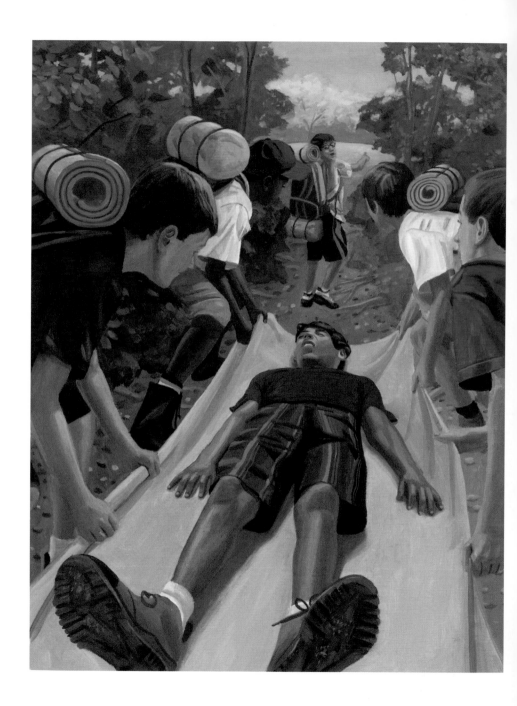

Zack took a deep breath. *This will work,* he thought. *It has to, for Ibrahima.*

"There are five of us, right?" Zack said. "So, that's two on each side of the tarp."

Erik nodded. "And one to take Point," he said, "to scout out the path so we'll know what's ahead."

Zack felt a rush of relief. Erik was more than solidly behind him on this; he was contributing to the plan. He looked at the other Birch Cabiners. "What do you think, guys?"

"I think it's a good plan," Jim spoke up right away. "You came up with it, Zack. Why don't you take first Point?"

"Everybody else good with that?" Zack asked.

One by one, the hikers nodded.

"Okay," said Zack. "Let's go."

"One, two, three, PULL! One, two, three, PULL!"

Zack's arms ached. And his back ached. He had no way of knowing how long they'd been dragging the tarp. But the sun was inching its way slowly down the sky. In just another couple of minutes, it would go behind the mountain. It would start to get colder. And darker.

At least it isn't raining, Zack thought. And the fact that the path was muddy had turned out to be a blessing in disguise. The wet ground made it easier to slide the tarp.

"Hey, you guys!" Kareem was Point and now he came dashing back to the main group.

"What is it?" Sean asked. "Trouble up ahead? Please don't tell me there's another landslide."

"No," Kareem shook his head. "Just the opposite. There's a clearing. I think it might be a good place to stop and rest."

"That *is* good news," said Erik. He seized an edge of the tarp. "One, two, three, PULL!" he said.

The tarp slid forward, the longest distance

on one pull yet.

It really helped, Zack thought, *to have a definite goal in mind—especially if the goal was a* rest.

"We made it!" Jim exclaimed a short time later. "Phew!"

"You can say that again," Sean said.

"We made it. Phew!" Jim repeated.

Sean groaned.

Making it to the clearing was helping everyone feel better. The light was fading fast, but the guys dragged Ibrahima to the biggest patch of sun. Now, they were going through their backpacks, checking out their food and water supplies.

"Anybody have an extra sweater or sweatshirt?" Zack called out.

"I have a sweater," Kareem said. He unzipped his backpack. "My mom made me promise to bring it on the wilderness trek. We never go back on a promise in our house. I've been feeling kind of stupid lugging it all this way."

"No, that's great," Zack said. He took the sweater and tied it around Ibrahima's head. Next, he spread his own sleeping bag over Ibrahima like a blanket. Ibrahima shivered, but said nothing. Then Zack asked, "Now, how about a pair of socks?"

"I can help with that," said Sean. "I brought *extra* extra socks." He brought his socks over and Zack slid them onto Ibrahima's cold hands. Sean went on, "We're dividing up the food. You should come and get some."

"In a minute," Zack said. He tried not to sound as nervous as he felt.

Erik came over and crouched next to Zack. He waited until all the other guys were busy putting on dry socks, gulping water, or eating. Then he said, "What's the matter?"

"I'm really worried about Ibrahima," Zack confessed. "He feels so cold. And I don't know about you, but I'm pretty tired, and so are the rest of the guys. It's getting dark. I just wish I knew how far away we were from help."

"We can't hike safely in the dark. Maybe we should camp here tonight," Erik began, "and then . . ."

"Guys!" Jim suddenly shouted. He was all the way across the clearing. "I think I see a light." Jim pointed. "There—through those trees. Hey! *Hey,* we're over here!" he yelled.

All of a sudden, everybody started shouting at once. Some of the guys dashed off down the path toward the light, waving their flashlights wildly and hollering as loudly as they could.

Then, "Aaaaoooo!"

The woods rang with a familiar howl.

"That's Cookie!" Zack shouted. "C'mere Cookie. We're over here, boy."

"Woof. Woof. Aaaooooo," Cookie answered.

A moment later, Cookie bounded into the clearing. Skeeter, P. L., and what looked like half the rest of Camp Wolf Trail were right behind him. Everybody was talking at once, swinging lanterns and calling out to one another.

Cookie launched himself straight at Zack.

Zack threw his arms around Cookie and fell back onto the ground while Cookie licked his face happily.

"When Carlos and the other hikers got back to camp and told us that you'd been separated from them, we didn't know which path you'd take," said P. L.

"We knew we'd need a good tracker," said Skeeter. "So, I told Cookie to come find you, and I knew he would." Skeeter smiled down at

Zack. "After this, I may have to change that rule about not feeding the dog. It turned out to be a very good thing that Cookie thought you sneaked that piece of bacon to him. When you dropped it, you didn't know it, but you were saving the day!"

Cookie bounded over and licked Ibrahima's face. Ibrahima opened his eyes and looked around.

"Ibrahima!" Jim shouted. "You're all right!"

"I have socks on my hands and a sweater tied around my head," Ibrahima said weakly, grinning a crooked grin. "How all right can I be?"

"Okay, everybody," P. L. said. "I'll save the speeches for later. But for now let me just say, great job. I am totally amazed and impressed that you guys made it this far. You really kept your heads."

"Yeah," Erik piped up. "And we used our heads for a change too. Thank goodness!"

"I can see that," P. L. said with a smile. "Now, the camp bus and van are waiting for us at the top of the next rise. The counselors will carry Ibrahima to the van and drive straight to the infirmary so that Doc Rosa can take a look at him. The rest of you, gather your stuff and head up to the bus. Dry clothes and a nice, hot, special late dinner are coming right up, soon as you get back to camp."

"What are we having?" Erik asked.

"What else?" Skeeter looked first at Erik and then at Zack and grinned. "Spaghetti and meatballs."

Chapter Ten

Later that night, Zack and Jim walked back to Birch Cabin. They were warm and dry, and their stomachs were full of their special late dinner of spaghetti and meatballs. Best of all, Ibrahima was safe and sound. He was staying in the infirmary overnight, but Doc Rosa said that he'd be just fine.

"Hey, guys!" a voice behind them called. "Wait for me."

Erik sprinted up. For several minutes, the three boys walked in silence.

"There's something I want to say," Erik finally burst out. "Actually, two things. Thank you, and also, I'm sorry. Really, really sorry."

"You're welcome, and what for?" Zack said.

"It's kind of hard to explain," Erik said. "I thought we were a great team today, didn't you?"

"I did," Zack said. "I thought we were awesome. I wasn't sure you'd want to do anything I suggested ever again after . . . you know . . ."

"But that's just what I mean," Erik said. "That's why I want to say I'm sorry. I really acted like a jerk, but you didn't hold it against me."

"Why would I want to do that?" Zack asked. "Besides . . ." He smiled at Jim. "That's what friends do. They don't stay mad at each other, right, Jim?"

"Right," Jim laughed.

All of a sudden, Zack stopped. Erik and Jim were so surprised that they kept on walking a couple of steps before they caught on. "What's

up?" Jim asked. "What's wrong?"

"Nothing," Zack said happily. "That's the whole point. I just suddenly realized that we still have the rest of this week and *all* of next week to go!"

"I know!" Erik said. "That is *the* best feeling."

"Yeah!" said Zack. He took a couple of running steps to catch up with Erik and Jim, thinking, *What's even better is the feeling that I'm right where I belong. At Camp Wolf Trail, with friends.*

REAL BOYS CAMP STORIES

Tom Gibian

Summer camp is both a place and a state of mind. Summer camp is for everyone, including you, whether you go to a real camp, or experience Camp Wolf Trail through this series, or even make up your own camp. Tom Gibian has known the magic of camp all his life. He started as a camper when he was a young boy, became a teen counselor, and served as a staff person as an adult. Tom is also the father of several campers and counselors. He certainly learned to love and appreciate children along the way. Now he spends most of the year as headmaster of Sandy Spring Friends School in Maryland. In his essay below, you'll learn that even after all these years, Tom still carries the joys of camp around with him every day.

Turn off the air-conditioning. Roll down the car windows. Take that first deep breath of sun-dappled mountain air.

You don't need a GPS to tell you that you're leaving behind the everyday world that's sometimes dull and predictable, full of handheld devices, microwaved meals, and yawns of boredom. You're climbing to where the air is sweet, coming nearer to the place

where you'll connect with yourself and recognize the best in others.

You're going to camp.

At camp, there are no report cards, no one really minds when you shout or sing at the top of your voice, ripped T-shirts are the height of fashion, and even the morning walk through the woods from your cabin to the dining hall is extraordinary.

You'll be sunburned, dirty, mosquito-bitten, and possibly without your toothbrush from the day you arrive. You'll find out that salamanders can be caught, held, stroked, and released. You'll climb up steep rock walls, paddle through white water rapids that bounce around boulders, and hike along narrow, twisting paths. You'll make so much noise at dinner that you'll practically raise the dining hall roof.

At night, around the campfire, you'll hear your friends tell stories about gigantic obstacles they've overcome, doubts they've blown to smithereens, fears they've stared down, friends they've supported, and high fives they've extended. And you'll tell your own great stories too. You'll feel unbelievably connected to your new best friend who is sleeping in the bunk above you, even when you don't know his last name yet.

You'll learn your camp's crazy and amazing traditions, like celebrating Christmas in August or smearing pudding all over your body and then diving into the lake. You'll figure out—without a dictionary or a guidebook—the wonderful, ever-changing vocabularies that are created, shared, perfected, and discarded to be replaced by other, different perfect words from one camp generation to the next.

You might set forth on ten-day wilderness trips carrying everything you need in a pack on your back. You might launch candle-carrying homemade boats that reflect their candlelight on the lake water during silent ceremonies.

Camp is the place where you'll experience homesickness for the first time. And, more importantly, for the *last* time, as you move toward independence, toward who you *really* are when you get to choose and to make decisions for yourself.

At camp, you'll find out what your own quirky, unique talent may be. You'll find it out noisily, happily, and naturally, not because you don't have any responsibility but rather because a lot is expected of you. Others will depend on you to find dry firewood, wash out pans in a stream, and divvy up food that you and your friends separately lug up and down trails until it can be collectively cooked, eaten, and thoroughly enjoyed. You can take on the responsibility of walking "Sweep" at the end of the line of hikers, which is a chance to make the slower kids laugh, the day-dreamers marvel, and the hustlers pace themselves while you point out a dozing rattlesnake or simply how sunlight comes through the tree canopy to light up the path.

The experience of camp is real and authentic, immediate, unfiltered, joyful, and spirited. Camp will change you. And when everything doesn't go as expected at camp, and you can be sure that it won't, you'll find out that forgiveness can be experienced in two ways—both given and received—that gratitude comes in waves, and that happiness is simple.

Stick the **ANIMAL TRACKS** card from the back of your book in your back pocket and start exploring!

Keep a lookout for animal tracks:

·in your yard ·in the park ·on sidewalks ·on the playground ·on the beach ·in the woods ·near a pond ·in snow.

Keep track of the tracks you see.

Use a felt-tip pen to put a check next to them on your TRACKS card.

Make tracks!

Kick off your shoes, get your feet wet, and make tracks yourself. Hey, you're an animal too!

Paws and Claws

Make your own track card by tracing or drawing your pets' paws. See if your friends can identify whose-foot's-whose.

Put Your Foot In It

Do this outside: Ask your friends to put their bare feet in paint and then step on paper. See if they can find their own feet.

Zoo-Do

Next time you go to the zoo, bring a pencil and some paper. Sketch any animal tracks you see. Better label them too!

Animal/Vegetable/Vehicle

Bikes, skateboards, leaves, acorns, bugs—all sorts of things leave tracks. In a small notebook, draw the most awesome ones you see.